CAMELLIA ENGKANTADA

VICTORIA CONLU

ISBN: 9798838063748

*For JB, because I promised that I would be a good example for you
in speaking up and telling stories that I feel should be told.*

CONTENTS

FOREWORD

Filipino folktales are full of mystical creatures, deeply intertwined with feelings of reverence and love towards the concept of home. Many of the most well-known tales in Filipino folklore – tales of the *aswang*, the *diwata*, the *engkanto*, the *dwende* – are rooted in the idea that the most ancient and most revered beings in existence are forever bound to protect their homes or recall their pasts. Many times, we imagine them and even represent them in movies and stories as very much like us, with conflicts and emotions that make them practically human. And this, perhaps, is why it was so fascinating to entertain the possibility of what it would look like if the beings of Filipino lore, much like the people themselves, were for a great many reasons uprooted from these homes and found themselves in new faraway lands where they are forced to begin new lives that are disconnected from the land and the circumstances that formed them.

The emotions that arise as a result of feeling far from home are the heart of *Camellia Engkantada*, and all of the stories that will follow in the series into the future. The stories of Filipino American families are built squarely on their immigration stories, the circumstances of individuals and of the world around them that drive them to the decision of leaving their homes and creating a new home. It is a theme that is the cornerstone of my family's own story, and I am sure that it is very much the same for many of yours. They are the stories we hear throughout our lives from our parents, grandparents, aunts, and uncles, of the circumstances under which they left the homes they knew for a different life, and a better life, a pivotal decision that would drive the stories of our families for every generation to come. We are who are and our lives are what they because of those very choices.

If the mystical aspects of our culture – the spirits and supernatural forests that were believed to have lived on the land of our grandparents and great grandparents – followed and were subject to these same forces, would they too feel the same longing, or the same struggle to balance the ways of both the old world and the new? The basic assumption of the stories you are about to read is that the answer to this question is, without a doubt, yes. How could they not?

The permanence and universality of this sense of missing home is well-suited to the idea of eternal, mystical beings, because the idea of home in and of itself is often an intangible one, wrapped up in memory and perhaps not always in truth – many times, the idea of home that we harbor when we have been far from it for a long time, or if it is a home we personally never knew but heard of in stories from those we love, is an image of something that may no longer exist. With these stories, I hope to capture in these beings of lore and myth a sense of humanity, and an attachment to the concept of home that remains frozen in time, even as we physically move through it.

1 ❖ ENTER THE DETECTIVE

The M-Town District, 1990's

Tch-tch-tch. Skreeeeee—

Detective Rico Montero – Monty, to most of his contemporaries – cringed at the sound of the waitress in front of him scraping food with a fork off of the sides of mixing bowl she had been preparing food in, probably dragging the utensil a little longer than she needed to in lieu of being able to voice her displeasure. He wondered where this lady thought she got off, being so obstinate with him. Sure, it was her job. Sure, he had come into her place of work during the morning rush and had immediately started asking questions. But he was working too, and in his mind, she was making his job this morning far more difficult than he would have liked. He was only responding in kind.

"I need you to tell me as much as you can, miss—"

"Detective," the waitress interrupted, her voice heavy with a sigh as she made no further efforts to mask her exasperation with him, only grudgingly pausing the task at hand. "I can tell you, I think a murder happening right outside is something I would have noticed, and if I didn't notice it, then the person must have known what they were doing. I can't imagine anyone who had gone out of their way to plan a whole *murder* would be that careless."

His intention had been to come into the diner this morning for quick answers and be quickly on his way, but this goal now appeared to be well out of his reach if the forty-five minutes he had spent here meant anything. What had he been expecting? Surely, he had thought, he should have at least been received ore graciously for the important work he was here to do… even if it seemed as though he was doing little more than chasing his own tail.

Perhaps he was just scrambling at this point for a lead to save face, or perhaps he couldn't accept defeat for the day. Whatever the case, he had wanted to leave the M-Town Diner with something – with anything.

But Monty admitted inwardly that the waitress who was busily preparing the M-Town Diner for its pending opening to patrons in less than an hour had a point – if she'd seen anything worth telling, she would have known it was worth telling without him having to pry it from her. The validity of the point, however, was muddled by the fact that she was so difficult to get answers from. Monty wondered if she was purposely being difficult, or if she was perhaps not the brightest. She just seemed so frank, so simple, he wondered if perhaps she was the tiniest bit dense, and if this was the reason he could not get any useful information from her.

The waitress, Camellia Ferrer, regularly pulled extra shifts at the M-Town Diner, a humble box of an establishment bookended by a bank branch on one side and a towering red brick apartment complex on the other. It was tiny and unobtrusive, one was likely to miss it unless they were actively looking, and while it never seemed to have a shortage of customers who passed through as they went about their busy days and nights, always seemed to struggle in finding adequate staff. As a result, Camellia was present from before the diner opened at nine in the morning, to after it closed at nine in the evening. This meant that if the coroner's examination was to be believed, she would have had to have been present when a businessman waiting for a cab nearby met his untimely end.

"Do you remember if this man ate in your restaurant last night?" Monty asked, walking over impatiently and holding out a photo of the dead man over the counter. "Maybe he had just finished eating here or something?"

"He might have," Camellia said, pausing and taking an earnest look. "But apart from the cook in the back – he never sees anybody – I was working the diner by myself last night, and there were customers in and out all night. There are customers in and out of here every night and I probably wouldn't remember any of them if I saw them again, especially this guy. There doesn't seem to be anything all that special about him." She paused, realizing most likely how insensitive she sounded, and added, "I'm sorry."

And it was a plausible reply – but Monty again for whatever reason wanted very much to be irritated with Camellia because it was not the reply he had wanted. Realizing that there was nothing he would be able to glean from this conversation with her, he thanked her for her time through gritted teeth and left in time to allow her to finish preparing for the morning rush.

It wasn't her fault really, he reminded himself as he made his way back to the precinct office, and he immediately felt a little guilty for having mentally berated her and thinking her dense in his irritation. It was just that this was his first major case – and potentially the case that would finally let him be called Detective Montero around the precinct. For now, that title belonged squarely to his father, a beloved retired detective with a reputation for shrewdness and the occasional run of pure luck that established his memory as the best of the best. Detective Francisco Montero, referred to lovingly as Montero the Elder since Monty's arrival at the precinct, was, for all intents and purposes, the stuff of legend, a young man raised by farmers who had come to the country without a dime to his name and made himself into something. A model. A savant in his profession. So, when he passed away just a few months ago, the line of people lined up to pay respects may have outnumbered the amount of people Monty had ever had a genuine conversation with at all.

Until Monty could prove himself worthy of sharing a name with that man, the one who had known simply as his father until he was forced to try and become him, he was simply Monty. It felt juvenile. It felt condescending. And maybe, if he could solve this case, he could finally rid himself of it for good.

The businessman found dead outside the M-Town Diner, as jarring and grisly as such a thing sounded, should have been a rarity and an anomaly here. In truth, it was actually the third in a series of unsolved murders in the past month, none of which produced any major leads as to who was doing such a thing in their precinct. While the neighborhood affectionately dubbed M-Town, a triangular crosshatch of inner city streets in the heart of the financial district, wasn't the nicest part of town by any stretch of the imagination, it certainly wasn't a part of town where you would expect something like this. M-Town was mostly home to a collection of shop and restaurant owners, its streets lined with alternating old immigrants pushing rickety wheeled carts and businessman skittering by in pressed suits.

"Any hints you could throw my way would be very much appreciated, Pa," Monty chuckled dryly to himself as he sat alone in his office, poring over the case file in its entirety for what had to have been the dozenth time since receiving it. But no guidance from beyond arrived. No supernatural intervention. No divine visions. Nothing…

"She was the most beautiful woman I had seen in my entire young life, and she said that if I would follow her into the woods, she would give our family everything we ever dreamed," an older man said as his young son settled into his lap. "She said that she would make the land burst forth with crops, and the animals would thrive and grow fat from the land, and we would have all the riches we ever dreamed of."

"And you told her no?" the young boy asked shrilly,

practically pouncing on his father to ask him for an explanation.

"Pa, are you crazy?"

"I had to say no. You don't accept gifts from the engkanto[1]."

"But why?"

৳

A little past two in the morning, from a bout of fitful sleep Monty awoke in a bit of a sweat – not because it was the dream of his childhood was a bad one, but because it seemed that his late father had paid him a visit in his dream, but without any assistance to provide. It was a fond memory he had dreamed of, one of many memories of late nights in his father's study listening to bedtime stories of the strange tales and beliefs from his father's childhood in the Philippines – a place that Monty himself had never visited, and admittedly, he held a fantastical, almost mystical view of the land of his family's origins – its small, humble farms, its lush forests crawling with vines and its ranges of fertile rolling hills – based on his father's

---

[1] In Filipino folklore, the *engkanto* are among many mythological creatures often associated with nature and the forest. They are said to bear striking resemblance to humans, but with extraordinarily slender, beautiful ,and even enchanting features that they often utilize as a means to draw in victims whom they are able to hypnotize, control, or otherwise cause events that can be positive or negative, depending on whether the individuals have either pleased or angered the *engkanto*.

retellings.

Montero the Elder seemed to always tell tales of his childhood that were simple, and magical – a kind of magic that came from history and nature that one simply did not find here. Maybe, Monty surmised, it was better that way. The world was messy enough without it.

2 ❖ CITY LIGHTS & FOREST GROVES

It took a full afternoon of obsessing over his case files, knowing that there was a bit of quiet heckling behind his back from his peers at his lack of progress, before Monty had reached a conclusion of any kind. The conclusion, however, was that he had spent over an hour yesterday harassing a young woman without reason – and he mentally kicked himself for having held her cold demeanor against her. He had just wanted so much to have a lead, any lead at all, that he had prematurely placed all of his hopes on her when all she wanted was to go about her day and finish her shift.

He would extend an olive branch, he decided, because there was still the possibility of her providing some value as a witness, or cooperating with the investigation in numerous other ways given the fact that all of the bodies happened to have been found within a reasonable distance from the M-Town Diner. If the killer struck again – and Monty almost hoped that they would, if only for the sake of making his first major case that much more of a victory – a pair of eyes that was on the scene practically every night would give him a leg up that he desperately needed.

So, this time with a much less haughty demeanor than he'd blustered in with the first time, he returned to the diner where Camellia worked, sitting down in one of the booths and waiting for her to come by.

"What can I get for you this evening?" she asked primly, not looking up from the order pad in her hand. "The special today is the French toast and bacon."

"Just a coffee, thanks," Monty said, reaching into his pocket and putting a twenty dollar bill on the table, drumming his fingers on the table to get her attention. "Keep the change. Consider it a peace offering."

"Your money isn't an apology, Detective. Not by a long shot. It's an insult." Illustration by Sumit Roy.

Camellia paused, looking back and forth with a deep, skeptical from between the money on the table and the strangely proud look on Monty's face, grinning and expectant as he awaited her response to his gesture.

"I'll be back with your coffee. And your change," Camellia said, snatching the bill off of the table and tucking it into the front pocket of her apron.

And that was, in fact, what she did. Camellia brought Monty his coffee and his change and didn't speak another word to him, instead busying herself in conducting niceties with all of the other patrons, so intentionally ignoring him that it could not evade his notice. So he waited – ordering refills on his coffee until the last few diners had cleared out of the M-Town Diner so that only he and Camellia were left inside.

"You sure don't know how to accept an apology," Monty finally spoke up while Camellia was behind the counter, polishing a tray full of drinking glasses she had just finished washing.

"I know how to accept apologies just fine. I never heard you offer one," she said, finally looking up calmly from what she was doing and allowing an exasperated sigh to escape, heaving at her chest. "Your money isn't an apology, Detective. Not by a long shot. It's an insult."

"You've gotta be kidding me."

"I'm very serious, Detective Montero," Camellia snapped back slightly, slinging her washrag over her shoulder. "You walked in here last night while I was working, you spoke to me like I was stupid because you knew I wasn't in a position to talk back to someone like you. And a coffee is a dollar-seventy-five. I'm not smart, I'm not educated, but I know how little that means you think my time is worth. How much of it do you think I have?"

Monty opened his mouth to protest but found only feeble attempts that crumbled before they left his lips. He had been demanding, even abrasive in his approach the previous night, he had even thought her dull – too dull to realize he was being condescending towards her.

"I don't make much here, Detective," Camellia continued. "But I'm not desperate enough that a twenty dollar bill can buy that kind of disrespect."

Stunned, Monty scratched the back of his neck and

gave a heaving sigh. Admittedly, in his mind, this was all more hassle than it was worth and he didn't feel that he had time to waste on a woman scorned. The fact still stood, regardless, that he was very much without any additional leads and could not afford to burn the only bridge he had in the case, even if this particular bridge was rickety and wasn't guaranteed to hold any weight, or get him much of anywhere.

"Listen, I'm… very sorry," Monty said, holding his hands up placatingly. "This is my first big case. I came in too hot, and it was a dumb move because I was here asking for your help. What can I do to make it up to you?"

"You can start by finishing your coffee and letting me close up for the night," Camellia retorted shortly. "I've worked two back to back shifts, and I'd really like to go home."

And because he did not want to risk further deepening the rift between himself and the only extra set of eyes he had right now in hopes of solving these murders, Monty had no choice except to oblige.

Camellia, as she walked home, felt herself agitated and restless in a way she never was – not in the normal way a young woman would be restless walking alone at night, as she had long grown accustomed to being alone this way. As she made her way down the city blocks back to the humble building where she rented a tiny flat, she felt a sort of crawling under her skin that she had not felt in years, a tightness in her chest that was so sudden that by the time she walked through her door, she shoved it shut behind her and leaned back against it, clutching her hand to her chest and taking a fair few deep breaths before she could manage to calm herself.

Had she been any less distraught, she might have been amused and even thought herself a little clever for having asked – how much time do you think I have? The right answer, after all, was one that the young man would have never believed even if she told him.

The passage of a great many years had dulled the edges of Camellia's anger. There were times that, being so accustomed to the humdrum of her new daily life, she forgot that any other life had once existed, as though she were merely going through a series of motions because she had drilled into her own mind that this – the daily drawl of waking up, walking to work, serving food all day, and doing everything over again – was what she had to do. She had come to this city so very long ago with such a singular purpose, it was unbelievable that she had practically forgotten it until her first direct encounter with the young detective they called Monty.

The morning after the murder had not been Monty's first time venturing into the M-Town Diner, nor had it been the first time Camellia had seen him – that day had been many months earlier, on an unseeming winter morning to have breakfast with his father, a retired detective that Camellia had only recently learned had since passed away.

"I'm proud of you," Detective Montero said to his son as Camellia placed their breakfasts down in front of them. There was a quiet hesitation to his voice that paired with his age made the sound itself seem dusty, and it was evident that these were words he did not throw around lightly. "You're going to be a good detective."

"Yeah, well," Monty chuckled, scratching the back of his neck while his father neatly and carefully cut his short stack of pancakes before drizzling on just the right amount of syrup – not a drop wasted. "I have a whole lot to live up to at the precinct. I've got your shoes to fill."

"You shouldn't worry about filling my shoes. I've walked too many miles in them, I'm sure they stink," Detective Montero chuckled, met only with a pause from Monty who did not appear nearly as amused by his father's joke. "It's not about how many cases you can close, or how many times you can call it a win," the older man explained after a pause. "Winning doesn't matter if you haven't done any good. And maybe, one day you'll crack a case that changes someone's life. Maybe one day you'll save a life. Those are the wins that mean something."

"I'm not going into detective work because it feels good, Dad."

"I'm not saying you should work toward what feels good, son," he said, shaking his head. "I'm saying you should work toward what feels right."

"Sure, dad," Monty replied, his expression strained as he struggled to really see the difference. He finished with an obliging but dismissive chuckle as he shook his head and took another bite of his breakfast. He seemed to quietly mull it over for only a moment, then he guffawed, gulping down a mouthful of scrambled eggs and dismissing his father's platitudes. "You just wait. There are hundreds of thugs and crooks out there with my name written all over their case files. All I need is a chance – all I need is one of these M-Town nobodies to beat up the wrong lady on the wrong night, and my career is set."

And hearing these grandiose ambitions, this still unfounded pride and peacocking, reawakened the anger that Camellia had all but forgotten – at men like Monty, and for her own reasons, Monty in particular. Monty's father was a principled man, of practically unimpeachable character whose only fault was perhaps that he could never understand why his son could not seem to easily behave in the same fashion. The elder Detective Montero, one of the few men for whom being truly good seemed easy, shook his head in disdain at his son's apparent disregard for the fact that these were people, not just case files, and Camellia could see the worry set deeply into the older man's features. And she felt for him. In fact, knowing the elder detective was such a principled, hard-working man, it was Monty's haughty, flippant nature that reminded Camellia so immediately of the reason why her quarrel with the Montero family existed at all. It was so many years ago, so many miles away in a place from which they were all now separated by a vast ocean and multiple lifetimes.

Many Years Earlier

"Lucio, huwag mo 'yan pakialaman![2]"

Lucio Montero, a tan-skinned and strapping gentleman with gracefully coifed jet black hair, grinned back at his beautiful wife, his small axe resting gently on one of his broad shoulders. Together, they had been taking a stroll across the land he had just inherited from his uncle, familiarizing themselves with the lay of the land and deciding where they would have their home built. Lucio and Lorena Montero had only been married less than a year, and were expecting their first child, so while his uncle's passing was indeed a sad event, it had benefited them in such a timely manner that they would have a perfect place to build

---

[2] Lucio, don't touch that!

their family home.

It had startled Lorena, who had grown up in a small provincial fishing town nearby as opposed to the city where Lucio had been raised, when her strapping husband made to take his axe to the overgrowth in the shrubs and plants ahead of them.

"Don't disturb anything. We're just passing through - nakikiraan lang po[3] --"

"Who are you talking to?" Lucio chuckled in spite of his wife's obvious distress at his flippant prancing through the woods. "You're so superstitious, mahal ko[4]."

"It doesn't do us any harm to be careful," Lorena said, wide-eyed and wondering as she stared around at their surroundings. "If there are spirits here, then they've been here forever and we arrived this morning. Why should we take any chances?"

But Lucio shrugged off her concerns and stepped forward a safe distance from her into the thicker brush, gesturing for her to keep a safe distance. He raised his axe and gave it a swing to clear the path, landing with a dull thud in the hearty trunk. Lorena gave a yelp, and Lucio used his free hand to clear away some of the loose brush to find that his axe had found its mark in the hanging limb of a large camellia tree.

---

[3] "Just passing through." In Tagalog, *po* signifies reverence and respect.
[4] My love

The tree was covered in white blossoms, and it had clearly been growing for many years without being disturbed, its limbs overhanging and tangled into the overgrown brush around it. Lucio gave a proud chuckle, while Lorena clapped her hands over her mouth to muffle a gasp. Lucio yanked his axe free and gave another more targeted, determined swing at the limb, severing it from the rest of the large tree and letting the branch fall to the ground with a rustle and a thud. He gave it kick with the bottom of his foot so the branch rolled aside, and he took a step further into the clearing to get a better look around.

"This is the area we'll clear for our home. It's perfect," Lucio declared proudly, stooping to place his axe down on the ground by his feet and pluck a white camellia bloom from the branch he had just cut. He stood and walked over, holding the blossom out to his wife with a grin, only to be met with hesitation from her. Her eyes were slightly widened, and she took a step back with her hands still clutched to her chest.

"Lucio," Lorena said, shaking her head. "You shouldn't have done that."

※

And perhaps, had Lucio listened to his wife's warnings to show the proper respect to all that had come before him to the small parcel of land he had claimed as his own, had Lucio stopped to consider that his uncle had owned this wild and unfettered land for decades while for very good reason leaving it undisturbed, he perhaps would have not have gone on to eventually uproot and destroy the years-old camellia tree - the namesake now of the vengeful spirit of nature who would never let him rest. Had Lucio listened, perhaps Monty's boastfulness could have been forgiven. Francisco – the elder Detective Montero, and Lucio's grandson – had gotten away with living to peaceful old age while Camellia watched and waited, only because he was pure of heart and deeply principled and Camellia could not bring himself to rain down the consequences of Lucio's actions upon him. The way of the ancient spirits bound to the land – of the *engkanto* – did not allow it, and so for an entire generation Camellia merely watched the man and his family from afar. She patiently and willingly stayed her hand

But in Monty, the long dormant anger within Camellia reawakened, in spite of the fact that by now, she had become strangely accustomed to the life she had adopted in following the Montero family across the sea to exact revenge for the forest Lucio had leveled for his own luxury. In Monty, Camellia saw the same pride that had doomed Lucio, and with familiarity came renewed fury.

3 ❖ PIECES INTO PLACE

Surrounded by piles of photos and tapes and boxes of evidence, Monty felt his irritation rising at the fact that he was having to start at square one in his attempt to determine if all of the M-Town murders had been committed by the same person when all that he had to link them was their physical proximity to one another. Besides this, all three murders while equally grisly were all very much distinct.

The man found at the wharf had died by blunt force trauma to the head and subsequent drowning. The man found at the rail station had died by strangulation. The man found in the alley across from the diner had died by apparent asphyxiation. All of the killings had been, for the most part, bloodless. The odds of them being completely isolated incidents were just as high.

So here Monty was, in search of something that would prove them to be related. Or unrelated. At this point, he wasn't even sure if that even mattered if he couldn't even solve one of them, let alone all three. He had settled on reviewing the surveillance tapes from the utility shed by the wharf and attempting to channel the intuition that his father was so well-known for. This spot was as good a starting point as any – there was no evidence of having had to transport the body, so something must have happened not far from where it was found. The estimated time of death had been late enough that little to no activity would be expected – by eleven o'clock, all of the maintenance and facilities workers at the docks would have clocked out for the evening. Monty surmised that no one suspicious would be lurking in the area so blatantly while employees were around to realize something was out of place, so he narrowed a timeframe of surveillance footage from an hour after the last employee left, to an hour after the murder – a total of eighty minutes.

In the eighty minutes of grainy, awkwardly angled footage, Monty was able to discern three vehicles in the immediate area, none of which he could identify with certainty but all of which had defining characteristics that he was able to note: a white pick-up truck with its bed covered by a tarp secured with electrical tape, a brown sedan with Mardi Gras-colored fuzzy dice hanging from the rear view window, and worn white van with rusted edges and patches where the paint had been buffed off completely.

It wasn't much. There was a high probability that it wasn't anything at all, Monty reminded himself, but he knew that he couldn't simply wait idly for a lead, even if it meant pursuing dead ends until something appeared fruitful. So, with nothing to go on except for three random vehicles, he turned his attention to the second murder case file.

The second victim – Monty had taken to referring to each of them as One, Two, and Three, respectively – was a bank employee at the main downtown branch, and Monty knew from witness interview that he normally left work at about 10 in the evening to ride the rail back to his home.

Two had been found dead in a locked supply room for the rail technicians that was accessible only by employee key card – the killer would have either had to be an employee himself, found a way to steal an employee's card, or had an accomplice. All key card swipes were logged by an employee ID number assigned to the card, and a review of the rudimentary logs gave Monty his first clue: Employee 4747.

He nearly knocked over his desk as he made a dash for the door. He nearly slammed right into the receptionist on his way out, nearly clipped every curb at every turn between the precinct and the rail station, only to be met with –

"Sorry – just give me a minute, it takes forever to pull up anything on these things..."

Monty had hoped his impatience wasn't showing as he waited for the shift attendant at the rail station to pull up their staff database, but he was undoubtedly anxious to try and find any lead that he could.

"That ID belongs to… Chuck Suarez. He's one of our electricians."

"Is he working today?"

"He's working practically every day," the attendant said. "Here, I'll radio him to meet you in the back office. One sec. Chuck!"

The attendee raised his walkie talkie receiver closer to his mouth and held down the button to speak over the crackling sound. Monty could already feel his palms warming and accumulating sweat in anticipation that this could be the guy. "Chuck, I have a detective here wanting to talk to you, can you meet him in the back?"

"Sure thing. Give me two minutes."

Monty's brow furrowed as he was led back into the back office – Chuck Suarez hadn't skipped a beat, hadn't sounded shaken at all by the prospect of a detective coming and asking to speak to him. When the tall, lanky man with tan skin and dark hair slicked neatly back finally made it back to join him, he reached out and shook Monty's had, looked him right in the eye.

"Can I help you with something, Detective?" Chuck asked. His expression was earnest and unguarded, his round eyes and unwrinkled forehead looking fully unperturbed.

"Detective Rico Montero," Monty corrected. "I'm

here for whatever information you may have about the murder that happened here not long ago."

"Shoot," Chuck said, letting out a low whistle. "I wish I had something for you. I left work and the next day, I come back and the supply closet is blocked off with crime scene tape so I can't even get to my tools or anything, so I'm wondering how I'm gonna get any work done –"

"You weren't working that evening?" Monty interrupted, walking around the desk inside the office so he stood behind it and leaned forward across the surface to continue speaking to Chuck. Maybe it was a little bit of a crutch, maybe it made him feel a little more in control of the situation when he felt like he was at the interrogation table, in his own stomping grounds. Whatever the case, control was something he was sorely scrambling for.

"Did anyone tell you it was your key card that last opened the door before the body was found?"

Stunned, Chuck raised his eyebrows and crossed his arms over his chest. "Shoot," he repeated, shaking his head. "I knew lost it. I just had to get that damn thing replaced the next day – I came in and had to ask Mary at the receptionist office to print me off a new one."

"You mean you didn't have the badge on you?"

"I stopped off at the bar to watch the game – I usually go straight home, but we usually never make the playoffs," he said with a slightly embarrassed chuckle. "I'll probably get written up for this, but I must've had a few too many beers and I bet that's where it fell out of my pocket without me even noticing. I didn't go anywhere else after work that night, that's the only place I can think of where it would've gotten lost."

"What bar was this?"

"Slammers," Chuck replied, gesturing with a jab of his thumb in what Monty had to assume was the direction of the establishment. "Best spot in town to catch a game – just gets crowded."

Monty muttered his thanks and some obligatory niceties to Chuck Suarez before letting him know he was free to go back to his work, while Monty headed back to his car to find the fastest route to Slammers.

Slammers. What kind of a name was Slammers, anyway? Monty wiped the sweat from his palms on the sides of his pant legs as he entered the bar, feeling admittedly out of his element, experiencing an uncharacteristic sort of hesitation as he walked inside and relief that in the early afternoon, no crowds had gathered.

It was not that he had no friends, or didn't know how to have fun, he reasoned with himself. Maybe he had missed out a little in his youth on simply being *young* in his relentless pursuit of being *someone*, developing achievements rather than interests, and this was why he rarely spent much time in places like this. It wasn't so bad, though, he observed as he straightened out his posture, drawing back his shoulders and resuming his usual cocksure strut as he made his way to the bar where the bartender appeared to be doing close to nothing with the mid-afternoon lull in business.

"Morning, Detective," the bartender said with a brief wave of acknowledgment once Monty flashed his badge. "Can I help you with something?"

"You just might be able to," Monty replied amiably, approaching the bar and taking a seat at the bar, resting his forearms on the edge and leaning forward toward the bartender. "Just trying to see if you can point me towards someone who knows anything about these murders."

"Gotcha," the bartender said, finishing drying one of his scotch glasses, placing it down, and slinging the dishcloth over his shoulder with a flourish. "Not everyday I get asked to help catch a serial killer."

Monty bristled at how flippant the bartender was towards all of this, biting his tongue to keep from the knee-jerk response to chide him. They could not have been distant in age, but in countenance, they could not have been farther apart.

"Right," Monty said, clearing his throat and giving as convincing a smile as he could muster. "I just need to speak with you about the night of… the big game?"

"The big game," the bartender chuckled, and Monty tensed, internally pleading that would not be asked which game he was talking about. "It was unbelievable in here that night. M-Town hasn't had a win like that in years, I remember that night like the back of my hand! Bumping the top ranked team this season out of the play-offs? What else could you ask for?"

"Yeah. The number one team," Monty chuckled uncomfortably, shifting his positioning seated on the barstool. "The…good old…"

He paused, and in a split second it became evident to the bartender, whose forehead immediately formed a small crease between his eyebrows, that he in fact had not found a kindred sports fan in the detective. "New Orleans?" he supplied as though this were the most obvious thing in the world. His expression fell when no sudden epiphany developed on Monty's face.

So much for rapport, Monty conceded inwardly.

"Look," Monty said, making a wiping motion with his hands. "A man lost his access key here that night, and whoever got their hands on it could very well be our killer. Did you have anything turned into the lost and found that your employees have access to?"

"Oh, man – we've got a lost and found, sure," the bartender shrugged, reaching under the bar and pulling out a small basket that he placed on the bartop. He gave the basket a small, jingling shake so Monty could get a good look at its contents: a few stray keychains, loose jewelry, an inhaler, eyeglasses…

"We don't get much turned in to the lost and found – everyone's usually a little too drunk," the bartender finished with an apologetic chuckle. "Too drunk to pick up your sunglasses, but not drunk enough to pass up a gold watch somebody else dropped. That's how we end up with most of this crap." Monty gave a groan in response.

"Was there anything unusual that night? Is there any way we could find out who was in and out of here?"

"We've got one camera, just one that sees everyone coming in and out the door, the cars parked right out front," the bartender shrugged. "There was a little tussle that night after the game – we had one New Orleans fan in here and it got a little loud once they lost and everyone had a few drinks in 'em. Nothing big. A couple shoves and the guy left on his own."

"Did you get it on tape?"

"Him leaving, yeah," the bartender replied. "We still have the footage stored on the computer in the back if you want to look it over. I'll get you set up."

The back office of Slammers was really little more

than a closet with a single desk and a chair with a computer set up, and the footage saved from the front door camera was nothing to rave about, but after a few minutes of fumbling through and looking for the right window of time, the bartender managed to find just the right window of time. A man in a denim jacket whose face was not clear enough to be identified walked into frame, clearly shouting angrily over his shoulder at whoever he had presumably just been in an argument with – he leaned over a nearby table to shout back one more presumed insult before a bartender could be seen shooing him away.

The man in the jacket sulked toward the front door of the establishment, and Monty leaned in close, attempting to make out some detail of the man's face to no avail. As his eyes scanned the frame, however, his hand immediately reached out to pause the video, and he again leaned in so that his face was practically pressed against the screen when he managed to catch sight of the car out front that the man walked out to – the familiar sedan with the fuzzy New Orleans Mardi Gras dice hanging from the rear view mirror. And this time, he realized with an enthusiastic pump of his fist, he had a license plate number that he could clearly make out – a positive ID.

"I think Mister New Orleans might just be our guy," Monty said with an incredulous laugh. "Well, shit. We might've caught him."

4 ❖ MEETING A MURDERER

In a way, Monty had come to believe, solving a case was a natural extension of his childhood for solving jigsaw puzzles. You always began far off in the margins, piecing together a vague idea of the image's shape and size. You pieced together the errant pair of fragments with no sense of where they belonged. But suddenly, somewhere as you slogged along and fumbled hopelessly with what seemed like nonsense, you happened upon the piece that formed one critical connection and from there the entire image seemed to come together so easily.

Such was the development of the M-Town murder case – the sudden discovery of the Mardi Gras sedan was the crucial connector piece. Now, as he waited for another officer to bring the identified owner of said sedan into the precinct for questioning, Monty could not repress the anticipatory twitching fingers and sweaty palms even amidst the gravity of the situation. Is this what it would feel like every time? Would it be the same rush every time he caught a hardened, dangerous criminal?

When the man of the hour was escorted in, however Monty felt jarred by the man's appearance. He was... nothing special. There was no suspicious gleam in his stare, no air of malice. For all of the pomp he had come to expect out of a moment like this, Monty suddenly had to shake the comedown of simply not feeling like he had caught a killer.

"Mister Salazar," Monty said, standing on the other side of the table from the man he had just spent the better part of three weeks trying to catch, only to realize that he felt woefully unprepared for this moment. This was supposed to be the crux of his investigation, wasn't it? This was supposed to be the moment you waited for in a mystery movie, where the tenacious detective grilled the murderer for answers and finally cracked a case wide open. "You know why you're here," he said in what he hoped was a commanding and confident tone. Monty hoped he knew. He wasn't sure how he would explain everything if he didn't.

"Because you think I had something to do with the dead man they found."

"Close, Mister Salazar," Monty said. "I'll be frank with you. I don't think you just had something to do with it. I have reason to believe you're the *only* one responsible for these murders."

"Murders?" Benny asked, his faced contorted in confusion and his hands tensing immediately where they rested on the table. "More than one?"

"Yes, Mister Salazar – we want to know what you have to do with all three murders this month."

"This month?" He parroted, as though speaking the words again forced them to make any more sense. His eyes flitted frantically, as though tracking a frenetic search through his own mind for any explanation, any memory, every sign.

"One at the train station. One at the wharf," Monty said, enumerating on his fingers each of the incidents whose crime scene photos and witness descriptions were now burned indelibly in his mind – though his voice quavered slightly, feeling slightly less confident at the sort of earnest confusion the suspect was giving. "And one across from the M-Town Diner."

The moments that followed would make Monty feel like the most naïve of rookies, but from the way the color drained from Benny Salazar's face, the simultaneous confusion and realization, the way he shook his head and struggled for words, he could just feel that he was not looking at a guilty man.

"No, no, no," Benny said in a doleful groan, shaking his head before burying his face in his hands. "No, no, that can't be where I was. That can't be why."

His tone was confused and mournful in such a raw, unrehearsed fashion that Monty couldn't help but feel in his gut that there was some truth behind it. He hesitated. Did he have the wrong man after all? But why would it gather this response from him? There was no denial, there was no resistance, just genuine and unabashed sorrow as though some part of him was not surprised. It was such a strange response, Monty had no choice, he needed to press the man further.

"Three weeks ago on Tuesday at the Market Street station, this man who worked at the bank was found dead," Monty said, opening the manila folder on the table and sliding a photograph of one of the murder victims across the table to Benny Salazar – the one to whom he had the most concrete link. "He waited at that same train stop every evening, someone who could have intended to harm him would have easily known where to find him. His body was found hidden in the custodial supply room the next morning. Can you tell me where you were that Tuesday evening?"

"No."

"Mister Salazar," Monty said shortly. "If you don't want to provide me with your alibi, then I can't –"

"I want to," Benny said, looking up mournfully, his eyes wide and flitting around in panic. "Sir, I want to tell you where I was, but I don't remember."

"You don't remember?" Monty raised an eyebrow, tilting his head to one side as though a change in angle would make any of this sound more sensible. "Did you have a lot to drink? After you got into that fight at

Slammers?"

"No," Benny said, shaking his head so violently, as though he too were desperate to make it make sense if it meant physically scrambling the memory back into his brain, as though he hoped it might have just been too securely tucked away and the violent motion would shake it loose from where it was hidden. "I mean, yes – I know I went to the bar. I went to watch the game."

"New Orleans was playing."

"My home team," Benny said with a doleful look up Monty. "I had been planning to go watch the game all week – I just… I don't *remember anything*," Monty said through gritted teeth, clenching his eyes jaw and giving himself a swift whack to the head near the side of his temple. "I want to remember," he said angrily with another thwack to his head. "I want to –"

"You have to remember something," Monty interrupted, his tone suddenly shifting in inadvertent nervousness at the sight of his primary suspect now practically knocking himself out – he was either a very desperate man, or a very good actor, and though Monty knew he should have probably learned his lesson about assumptions when he'd first insulted

Camellia, he couldn't shake the thought that Benny Salazar was just too simple-minded to be a good liar. But if he was a bad liar, the remaining possibility was that he was in fact a victim. And if Benny Salazar was a victim, the question then remained: a victim of what?

⚘

The lunchtime rush at the M-Town Diner had already subsided when a young man plodded in, his shirt disheveled and a clipboard tucked underneath his arm. Slightly winded, he glanced around until Camellia gestured for him to take a seat anywhere while she finished setting up to brew another pot of coffee.

"Late lunch today?" she asked cordially, grinning politely as she walked over and pulled her order pad from the small pocket in her apron. "It looks like you've been working pretty hard."

The young man looked down at his rumpled shirt that had come half-untucked and wiped his slightly sweaty palms on the front, smoothing out some of the creases and using his elbow to slide his clipboard out of the way just enough. "I guess so," he admitted with a bashful chuckle.

"What can I get for you?"

"A cheeseburger would be great. And a coffee."

"Coming right up," Camellia said. As she tucked her order pad away into her pocket again, she took a glance at the papers on the young man's clipboard: a stack of papers with lines of signatures, and a few pamphlets featuring photos of a man whose features she recognized. It was a feeling she had of course felt many times before – she had been around so long, and had seen so many people, many faces seemed to bleed together nowadays. That was the funny thing about living through several lifetimes, the people almost seemed to repeat themselves, as though life were some kind of revolving door. "Some kind of petition?" Camellia asked, nodding towards the rustled stack of papers.

"A few things. Getting people signed up for our mailing list. Getting people signed up to vote," the young man said, now gently moving the clipboard closer again so it was more easily in Camellia's view, seeing his opportunity and likely thinking that asking couldn't hurt – it couldn't be any worse than some of the more brusque refusals he'd been on the receiving end of today. "Are you signed up to vote in the fall?"

"What, me?" Camellia asked with an incredulous expression, her forehead wrinkling as she scoffed at the thought. "I'm a waitress. I leave the politics to the professionals."

"I've heard that a lot today," the young man admitted with a chuckle. "But, hey, take one of these just in case. I'm working for Senator Ka's campaign, and he really wants to do some good things. Good things for regular people, not just –"

"*Ka?*" Camellia asked, taking the pamphlet that the young man had pulled from his clipboard to give to her. She studied the face of the man on the pamphlet who had already seemed familiar, and glanced over his slogan. Lorenzo Ka. *Ka Para Sa Kapwa*[5].

Her lips pursed, and her eyes narrowed slightly at the use of their mother tongue – something dearly preserved in their community, especially among the older immigrants who still lived here – and she felt a strange sort of irritation at it. What was this man getting at? Exploiting the longing that so many of them

____

[5] Roughly in this context, *Ka, for His Fellow Man*

had for home in order to get their votes? Exploiting the young seeking out some sort of connection to their roots to advance his own career?

If that was the case, Camellia thought with her face growing more and more stern as her mind became more and more critical of the man on the pamphlet invoking the spirit of *kapwa tao* – of care and connection to his fellow man – for the sake of politics. He looked young – he could have been no older than forty and more than likely didn't know any better than to believe such things. She scoffed and politely slid the pamphlet back across the table.

"What would he know, anyway?"

"I don't know – he seems like he knows what he's doing, you know?" the young man supplied. "Like he's seen so many things. I've met him – he cares about people. Especially the people here in M-Town. You know when they wanted to tear down the apartments on Ketterman Street?"

Camellia's brow again furrowed in recognition of the street name – a few years back, it had been the site of a large protest. An old apartment building on the corner had long been home to a large group of the community's working immigrants, many of whom lived alone without family and spent their days going back and forth between work and their small flats. It had been threatened some time ago to be sold off to a land developer to turn into a movie theatre and shopping space, before the project was stopped by massive protests. Camellia remembered it well for the droves of people who flooded into the diner for food, riled up about something happening in their neighborhood in a way that Camellia had rarely seen otherwise. She remembered the lunchtime rush. And she remembered feeling for them dearly, knowing all too well the feeling of losing a home.

"Senator Ka organized that protest," the young man at the diner table supplied, seeing the brief moment of openness in Camellia's face. For a moment, she glanced back at the pamphlet, especially focusing on Senator Ka's photograph. Perhaps that was where she had seen him before, Camellia pondered. Perhaps he had been there in the diner. "He seems… like an old soul, I guess."

This was enough to snap Camellia back to reality, and again she scoffed at the young man's idealistic views, laughing gently as she patted him on the shoulder. "And what would you know about old souls?" she asked, humored and indignant at the thought the young man in front of him could have any concept of a life long enough to span generations. Centuries. "I'll go get you your cheeseburger."

The case was solved, and that should have been something that felt like a victory to Monty – it was no small feat to say that one of his first major moves as a full-fledged detective was catching a serial killer. By every objective measure, Monty was an immense success and had proven himself just as competent as his father.

And yet it lingered, etched indelibly in his mind how Benny Salazar wept when he was shown the blurry footage of himself dragging the obscured body of the businessman away from the back lot of the M-Town Diner, as though it were an unexpected sight. He was a good actor. He was simply mourning being caught. All of these theories were things Monty had already considered, even forced himself to try to believe as he tried to turn the page on this case, and yet he could not.

That was why he found himself back at the impound lot where they were still holding Salazar's car. There were still answers to be found, and Monty couldn't accept the accolades for his success until his success was definitive, until his achievement was without question. The spectre of his father's prowess loomed large over his victory. Detective Montero the Elder had set the lofty precedent that cases and mysteries were either solved or unsolved. He had set the expectation that a Montero should solve a case *well* on the principle that nothing was of greater value than integrity and veracity. To Monty, the principle was trite, but the precedent was law. If he could follow the rabbithole of the Benny Salazar case to its very bottom, if he could not find the ultimate cause and solve this case *well* the way his father would have, he could never be satisfied.

Benny Salazar's old brown sedan had accumulated a layer of dust over its interior in the short time it had been sitting in impound but overall spoke volumes about the man's life with candor that could only be gleaned from a glimpse of someone's everyday routine.

It was relatively clean, with a plastic bag of garbage neatly kept hanging off of the headrest on the passenger side. In the back seat, there was a jacket and a spare pair of tennis shoes, nothing suspicious or incriminating. It wasn't the dirty, disheveled mess that Monty had come to associate with drug addicts and drifters who lived out of their cars. Benny Salazar was just a man who worked a couple of jobs and picked up odd small gigs here and there to make ends meet, which meant from time to time, he changed in his car and ate in his car. Nothing out of the ordinary, and more notably, nothing particularly criminal. But, Monty reminded himself, one could leave no stone unturned, no assumption unchallenged.

Monty slapped on a pair of gloves and first began rifling through the trash bag, finding nothing of interest. Wrappers for hot food from the convenience store, an empty pack of cigarettes, nothing that seemed to point anywhere except to the busy life of a man doing his best to survive in a world the Monty knew was not a kind one. If anything, it made him feel even worse about the conclusion of this case, because the more he looked into the life of Benny Salazar, the more he became a regular man, a humble man in worn shoes does what he needed to get by. Just like his father. It almost enraged him now, realizing that in this situation, the man most similar to Detective Francisco Montero was in fact the man getting put behind bars, not the man solving the case.

Perhaps more forcefully than was warranted, Monty reached next into the back seat and grabbed the worn out jacket. Checking the pockets, he finally found something out of the ordinary – a receipt for the M-Town Diner dated weeks before the murders began, and a flower. It was a hearty white blossom that should have been dried and withered by now for how long it had been sitting in a dark coat pocket but was instead pert and lush and full as though it had only just been picked.

It defied logic and it was unsettling because of its potential to lead down a rabbithole he would look like a fool explaining to his peers. So, Monty was gravely tempted to ignore it. What was he going to say back at the precinct to justify following this hunch? That he found a magic flower in a serial killer's car and it had given him such a funny feeling that he deigned it worthy of wasting city time and tax dollars? He would be laughed at.

But he also knew that letting this go was not what his father would have done. His father's sparkling reputation was maintained in part by the fact that he never gave a damn about it. He was so righteous and single-minded in his pursuit of truth that he never cared about being laughed at, and in turn, because he was practically always right, he was never laughed at anyway. Monty could not bring himself to feel the same way, to have the same dismissive nature towards the opinions of his contemporaries. But the feeling of being a lesser man than his father won out, every time. He needed to talk to Benny Salazar at least one more time – even if it was nonsense, even if it led nowhere. It would allow him at the very least to close this door once and for all.

Salazar, now dressed in an inmate's jumpsuit when brought out to meet Monty in the interrogation room, had lost weight in the time he had spent in custody, appearing gaunt and scruffy and altogether disoriented.

"Mister Salazar," Monty said as the man sat down at the table across from him. He placed a plastic bag on the table contained the large white blossom from the coat pocket, and the receipt. "Shot in the dark," Monty said in a low voice, leaning across the table. "Tell me everything you can remember about this flower. I found it in your coat pocket."

Handcuffed, Salazar awkwardly reached over and slid the bag closer to his side of the table and looked down at it. "That's right, I ate at the diner a while back. It was a little out of the way, but I had just finished repairing the back fence at the bus terminal parking lot and I had been at it all day so I was starving. Some guys were hassling the waitress there while she was trying to work so I scared them off. She didn't have any money on her, so she gave me this flower to say thank you. It was a sweet gesture."

A sweet gesture. Monty maintained his poker face, but he struggled to bite back a response of how much he doubted that.

"It's nice," he said in what he hoped was a casual tone. "What kind of flower is this?"

"I'm pretty sure this is a camellia. I don't see too many of them growing around here," Salazar said, before chuckling in a half-hearted attempt to make light of the situation. "Why? Looking for ideas for a particular lady?"

"Something like that," Monty said with a forced grin. "Listen, you hang in there. I think we still have some questions that I need answered, but you're not the one who can answer them for me."

Part of why his father gained such a reputation and was so revered was that so much of his work was done on gut feelings and intuition – but Monty prided himself on being a disciple of logic and intellect, or not needing to rely on such things. This case, this lead, however, seemed to fly in the face of everything Monty based his detective work on. When it came to the Benny Salazar case, the only logical conclusion that he could reach was that there was something at play that defied any semblance of logic. That was what kept Monty up at night, fixated on this case, and now it was what had him driving across the city close to midnight to the M-Town Diner to find out what Camellia Ferrer had to do with Benny Salazar and these murders once and for all.

Monty parked his car in the back lot of the diner and for a few minutes, sat in his car with the lights off, almost struggling to stomach what he was doing. He reached into the glove compartment and pulled out the plastic zipper bag that contained the camellia blossom and the receipt for Benny's meal at the diner, staring at the items under the flickering light of the rickety parking lot lamps. This was going to sound foolish, he said, cringing in the darkness and shaking his head. What had he come here planning to do, barge into the diner and tell this woman who had already been ruled out as a suspect that he was sure she was responsible somehow because he found a flower she shared a name with? He had simply rushed here with a foolhardiness that was completely unlike him, without a badge, a gun, or a warrant, and expected something to come of it.

What was happening to him? What could he even do with this? To what end? Even if there was some kind of connection, now that he thought it through, it was nothing he could take to the bank – or to court. He was as good as dumping all of this time and energy into the trash for all the good it would do him. What the hell was the district attorney going to do with this? What could they prove beyond a reasonable doubt when anyone with an ounce of reason would have plenty of doubt?

The Elder Montero could have done something with this. Detective Francisco Montero, or at least the version of him that existed in everyone's memory, could have taken this sad excuse for evidence, a paperclip, and a shoestring, and turned it into a case that saved an innocent man's life. But Monty was not his father, he decided, shutting his eyes and letting out a loud groan, and he was not going to act on this stupid gut feeling trying to prove that he could be. This was ridiculous. Benny Salazar had committed the crimes, magic flower or no magic flower, and made no attempt to pretend he had not been behind them. He was ridden with guilt and wanted to do his time, because he had killed the men who had been popping up around the city, end of story. Anything Monty would try to extrapolate was a flailing, desperate attempt to make this case more interesting than it was – a drowning man looking at the life raft presented to him and foolishly wishing he could find another one more to his liking. He was not that desperate to prove himself, he convinced himself. Letting out another breath, he finally opened his eyes and moved to start his car and leave before he made a complete idiot of himself.

When the headlights came on and before he could start the engine, however, the yellowish-tinged lights revealed a figure standing in front of his car, unmoving and relaxed as though they had been standing in the same place for a while, just watching.

"Camellia."

Finally, she moved, undoing the waist tie of her work apron and pulling it off over her head, draping it calmly over her arm before returning to her silent, direct gaze into Monty's eyes.

"Camellia," he said, leaving the keys in the ignition just in case while he opened the car door and stepped out, maintaining eye contact with the woman the whole time, neither of them yielding to the other, though Monty struggled to focus directly on her against the backdrop of the yellow streetlight flickering overhead at an erratic staccato pace.

Camellia's lips quirked into a nearly imperceptible smile at the sight of Monty's exhausted features and rumpled clothes, amused with the knowledge that she was wearing him down. Had he not eaten? Had he not slept? Had the inability to find the truth driven him nearly mad? She hoped it had.

But the amusement, Camellia had already realized, was always short-lived. There was fleeting sort of glee each time she saw Monty's frantic attempts to make sense of everything she had put into motion, but it was nowhere near the vindication she thought she would feel. Fleeting inconveniences were not retribution.

In the weeks since Monty came to speak with her, Camellia was reminded of her purpose. Comeuppance for the Montero family would not be achieved through one silly unsolvable case. This was not enough in exchange for everything she had lost and endured.

"I'm going to need you to answer my questions," Monty said sternly, keeping his distance from the woman, the distance between them thick with tension despite the crispness of the autumn evening air. "You had something to do with this, didn't you?"

"Your father would have followed his instincts to me much more quickly," Camellia replied with a slight shrug of her shoulders.

"When Benny came, you spoke to him."

"I did."

"What else did you do?"

5 ❖ DUBIOUS GIFTS

Months Prior

"We gave you three weeks, Salazar. Much longer and we're gonna expect you to pay back with interest."

Benny Salazar had not intended to go this long without paying back his debts. It was supposed to be a couple weeks – he'd made a deal with Dubose that he could have a small share of his most recent stash to sell for some extra cash, he would pay back a set price regardless of what he made off of it once he was stable. But the extra cash on hand was too tempting. It was innocuous at first, paying his rent and getting some much needed car repairs done. Then, while he still had the money, it was new tools since so many of his side gigs had been handiwork and repairs. No malice, but all irresponsibility. The money was simply there, until it wasn't, and now when Dubose was coming around to collect, there was nothing left.

Benny had been picking up extra jobs here and there to try and make any amount of it back, including odd repair jobs around the city by people who had been told by word of mouth that he would do them for cheap. It just never seemed to be enough to get caught up when he still had bills to pay and a stomach to fill, and when Dubose came around to inquire just as Benny was finishing up a job and heading to the diner for a quick meal, he was wholly unprepared to face him. He wasn't running from his debt. He just needed time, but even time nowadays cost a pretty penny.

"I can settle for a down payment," Dubose said, "Whatever you got. I just need to be assured that I'm gonna see what I loaned you back in my hands. Nothing personal."

"This is all I can give you right now," Benny said,

rifling through his pants pockets for his wallet and producing a couple hundred dollars – not even half of his debt. Dubose snatched the money out of Benny's hands and looked down at it, unimpressed.

"I did you a favor, Salazar," Dubose said sternly. His hand drifted to his coat pocket, and Benny tensed, knowing that forgiveness of a debt was a kindness rarely afforded to people like him by people like Dubose. "I got people I need to answer to too. I'm gonna need to see that money back, and soon."

"I'm working on it."

"Working on it isn't a reassurance, Salazar. Working on it doesn't pay off a debt," Dubose said. "You can't run out the clock on this one."

"I'm not trying to, Dubose, I swear. I –"

"Excuse me."

Both men looked up at the sound of the tinkling bell that was perched over the main door to the M-Town Diner and saw that the waitress inside had pulled it open and peered out at the two men speaking outside.

"My manager says I can't have people loitering around out front. Are you two coming in here or not?"

Benny paused, looked back and forth between Dubose and the waitress, and immediately came up with a plan to get himself out of this. "Wait here," he said just loud enough for Dubose to hear. "I'll have your money once I get through with dinner. Just hang around."

Dubose's face went blank, clearly not fully confident in Salazar's promise. "Enjoy your dinner," he said with a slight scoff, glancing back at the waitress who had witnessed their exchange one more time before walking off in the opposite direction.

It was shameful, what he was thinking of doing — Benny was ashamed of himself for even considering taking advantage of the kindness of a girl who had had gone out of her way during her shift to get Dubose off of his back. But bad things happened to undeserving people sometimes — it was how the world worked. He just had to hope that the world would be a little fair and make sure this girl caught a bigger break later.

The girl gestured for him to sit at any of the open tables, and she came by shortly after with a pot of coffee and her notepad. She placed the coffee pot down on the table, pulling a pencil out from the small pocket in front of her apron.

"This pot is cold already, been sitting for a little while," she said with an apologetic laugh. "I'll just toss this one out and put a new one on if you'd like some."

"Water's fine," Benny said. "But a slice of the key lime pie would be great. Would you let me help you clean the place up? Just to say thank you for getting that guy off my back."

"That? That was work," the waitress said, waving her hand dismissively. "We have to shoo people away all the time if they look like they're up to no good."

"Miss, I really –" Benny began, reaching out as though to stop the waitress from writing down his order, but in the process knocking the pot of coffee off the edge of the table with his sudden movement. With impressive speed, the waitress managed to catch the container before it hit the ground and shattered, but not before its contents spilled all over her front.

"Crap! Oh, no," she said dolefully, he arms extended partially as she looked down at the splash of hours-old coffee splayed over the front of her apron. "At least it wasn't hot –"

"God, I'm so sorry. Please, go get cleaned up, this

is all my fault."

"Thank you – I'll be right back, sir, I'll get you that pie while I'm back there," Camellia said apologetically, scurrying off to the back of the restaurant.

When the doors closed behind her, Benny took a look around briefly to make sure there were no errant passersby outside the window before making his way behind the counter. He made quick work of getting the register open grabbing a large a fistful of cash as he could manage, and gently sliding it back shut. He returned to his seat with a formidable amount of cash in his coat pocket by the time Camellia came back out with a fresh work apron and a slice of key lime pie.

"No harm, no foul," she said with a smile, placing the place with a freshly cut slice of pie down in front of him. "Can I get you anything else?"

"No, no," Benny insisted. "You've been such a sweetheart. You have no idea."

And indeed, he felt his insides churning at the idea of having done what he just did to such a nice young woman. But that was the way of things – sometimes, he repeated, unfortunate things happened to people who had done nothing to deserve them.

He had no idea how true that would turn out to be, or that ultimately it would himself on the receiving end.

Camellia gave a slight yelp once she had looked up and taken a glance out the window to catch a glance of Dubose again, standing outside and staring at them. "What is he doing back here?"

"I'll take care of this, don't worry about him. Stay here," Benny said, getting up from his seat and walking out the door to meet Dubose on the sidewalk. "Hey, if you're not here to order something, you need to get moving," he barked loudly, making a motion like he was attempting to usher Dubose away from the entrance to the diner, but as he did so, he transferred the cash from his pocket to Dubose's. They shared a furtive nod.

"Alright, alright," Dubose replied loudly, his voice barking and abrasive with a forced lilt made to sound as though he were just some drunk. "Just hanging around to see if you had some spare change."

And as he walked off, Benny returned inside to where Camellia had been watching, dusting off his hands as though he had just completed some task.

"He shouldn't be bothering you anymore," Benny

said, drawing his shoulders broad and nodding in satisfaction.

"You're too kind," Camellia said, smiling warmly in return. "I don't have a lot, but here. I want you to have something. Consider it a gift."

"You don't need to do that, miss."

But despite his feeble protests, Camellia reached out and placed something in his hand – a hearty, white camellia blossom.

꙼

"Where your family comes from, there's a story, isn't there? I'm sure you know the one," Camellia asked quietly, tilting her head to one side. Something in her voice and her demeanor, however, seemed far from the humble waitress that had first been identified as a potential witness in the Salazar case. Her voice was airy, taking on an almost ethereal quality, simultaneously softer and somehow more wild. "A story about the spirits that live in the trees and the water and flowers, that if you accept a gift from them…"

Her voice trailed off and Monty looked down, muttering quietly to himself. Hadn't Pa told him these stories before? About the spirits that lived on their land? It flooded back into Monty's brain, the way he used to sit with his father in the study and listen to these tall tales.

And perhaps it was just a trick of the flickering streetlamp above them, or perhaps a trick of fatigue and desperation. Whatever it was, for a moment, when Monty tried to focus his gaze on the woman in front of him he instead could have sworn he saw a different figure entirely – still a woman, but taller, ethereally pale with glowing eyes, and dark hair that was wild and flowing as though caught in an undying, unfelt breeze.

For a flicker of a second, Monty could have sworn he saw the same figure from the stories he had so often dreamed of as a child, the figures of the land of his father that had once fascinated him so deeply and whose stories he had begged to hear into the wee hours of the morning while nestled into his father's old armchair. Desperate to clear his mind of such nonsense – there was no way he could have seen any of these things, because he had learned long ago that they were stories for children that old men told to get them to behave – he shook his head violently, and his sight again focused to see the woman in front of him, the caramel-skinned and dull-haired woman in a waitress apron. She was plain, and humble, and nothing to be afraid of in the slightest. Whatever he had just seen was a trick of the eyes, and nothing more. It had to be.

"That would be absurd, wouldn't it?" Camellia finally asked with a quiet chuckle, knowing full well the stories that Monty's father must have told. "A man of logic such as yourself would never believe in that sort of thing, would you?"

She was taunting him, Monty realized. None of this made the least bit of sense, yet somehow was also the piece of information that made everything make sense. Benny Salazar failed to remember any of the murders because while he had physically committed them, it had never been him in control. He had accepted a small gift from Camellia and in turn, she was able to enact her will through him.

"That means," Monty said, his brow furrowing as though he were angry at himself for even arriving at this conclusion, as ridiculous and illogical as it was, "that you're an *engkanto.*"

"You remembered, Rico," Camellia said with a

quiet laugh that seemed to bounce and echo almost melodically off of the blacktop around them. "Your father would be so proud of you, wouldn't he?"

But her words were laced with derision, of which Monty immediately felt the sting. If she knew as much as she seemed to, then she knew that living up to his father's legacy was his single-minded pursuit – and she knew that thanks to her intervention in his first big case, he would always fall short.

The idea caused a rumble of rage to build in the pit of Monty's stomach, knowing that he had the answers he sought in this case, and he could never do anything with them. He could not simply cuff her and present his colleagues with the explanation that he had arrested her on the accusation that she was some kind of forest fairy who was committing the murders through Benny Salazar with mind control. He would humiliate himself, and this was the choice he was presented with: public disgrace in the name of doing the objective right thing, or the knowledge for the rest of his days that the first chance he had been given to prove himself a man as good as his father, he had knowingly and willingly fallen short.

He was forced now to acknowledge that he was not as selfless a man as his father was. Francisco Montero would have fought to prove Benny Salazar's innocence at any expense if he knew as much as Monty did. Monty, on the other hand, simply could not stomach the possibility of being the laughingstock of his peers.

And he immediately knew that as much as he purported to be a man of logic and not of emotion, the emotion he felt in this moment was clear: he hated Camellia Ferrer. She had been a blank slate, a cool, still pool of water that sat waiting for him to show signs of his own fallibility, then showed him his reflection and pulled him in to drown in it.

So, as was the instinct of a drowning man, Monty fought against the waters pulling under out of a blind, instinctual desperation to survive. He lunged towards Camellia, knowing that at least in physical strength, he could overpower her. He underestimated the strength that accompanied decades — over a century of repressed rage. So every strike he landed, she met with equal fury and precision. The knife in her hand found its mark in his side, but he barely felt it in the heat of the moment, taking advantage of her hesitation to grab a hold of her wrist.

He wrenched her wrist back until the knife fell to the ground with a clatter and he scrambled for it, and again blow for blow they met one another until both fell to the ground, bloodied with the knife skittering out of both of their reach.

Monty appeared to have expended the full measure of his strength in their confrontation. He lay still with his eyes shut and his breaths shallow. Camellia, on the other hand, was not yet prepared to succumb, and she felt power in her yet – enough, at least, to finally achieve what she had long planned. Wincing and clutching her side, she made an attempt at getting up to finally bring all of this to what she had considered its inevitable end. When she found, however, thar her current fragile human form could not yet manage the task of getting back to her feet, she fell to the ground with an agonized groan. Was this where the long road she had walked for so long truly ended, just short of its planned destination after over a century of traveling? For the first time in so many years, her mind finally drifted back to a time before all of this – a time before the Montero family's path ever crossed hers.

6 ❖ THE TALE IS TOLD

There was a time long ago, when the land was still left alone in its purest form, that Camellia had been young, had roamed freely and peacefully among the engkanto who imbued life upon the forest. Their presence breathed life into the forest, and in turn its natural wonder sustained them for centuries, allowing them to watch saplings grow and rise into the sky, to watch vines crawl along the forest floor, to watch the birds hatch and grow and fade away the way all other living things did.

Of all the other beings that dwelt in their forest, Camellia was closest to the older and wiser being called Kawayan. Kawayan was the engkanto that tended to the hearty bamboo grove that thrived at the forest edge. Tall, slender, and fair in color like his namesake, he often told Camellia, who then was so much younger and softer and wondrous towards the world outside their sanctuary, tales of things he saw from high above. He saw cities and roads, and many other things that they never believed would come into their midst, while she sat on a large rock in the sun, mouth slightly agape in wonder.

"Those things will never be close enough for us to get a real look at," Kawayan had told Camellia one day while she listened wide-eyed and amazed about the things he saw beyond the forest.

"That's alright – it's nice just to hear about them," Camellia shrugged dismissively. "What would need any of those things for, anyway?"

To the engkanto, there was no sense of ownership or borders to their land, and therefore no inkling that these faraway things would ever come to commingle with them. There was no awareness of the concept that a person – one single man – could be given a piece of paper that said that by the laws of his kind, this place was his regardless of what already inhabited it. And so, when the piece of paper passed into the hands of Lucio Montero, what came next was so jarring that only now, centuries later, did Camellia truly understand what it had done to her.

It was Kawayan who tended to Camellia's wounded arm, having carefully applied a poultice over the deep cut that had appeared when Lucio severed the limb from the flowering bush in the forest clearing that Camellia guarded. She remembered her good friend's sharp and slender features wrinkling in concern as he realized the distant visions they so fondly talked about here in their home were no longer anything quite so distant.

"But they wouldn't be arrogant enough to assume that this stops being our home just because they've decided it's theirs, would they? That has never been the way!" Camellia asked shrilly in disbelief, hissing slightly in pain as Kawayan's hands pressed over her wound, sending a warming sensation through the injured limb so that in a brief few seconds, the wounded flesh was healed over with new, pink skin that was pearly and scarred, but intact.

It was only a matter of days before Lucio returned with men he had hired to clear the area with torches and axes, tearing down the vines and trees and brush that had covered the land for centuries, terrifying away the creatures who had made their homes inside amid the undergrowth. Both the creatures and the forest spirits dispersed in their terror, some of them falling as the trees and plants they protected were forcefully torn from the earth. Camellia, attempting to flee alongside Kawayan, felt a sharp pain and looked back over her shoulder to see one of Lucio's hired men hacking away at the years-old camellia tree. She felt herself grow dizzy and drop to her knees, with Kawayan yanking on her arm and attempting to drag her to her feet.

"Camellia, please, come on," he said, giving her arm a pleading shake. "Get up."

But she didn't have the strength to stand. She didn't even have the strength to keep her eyes open for much longer than a few seconds. Instead, she felt herself crumple to the ground, drinking in a last glance at the forest as it succumbed to the destruction.

"It was only a matter of days before Lucio returned with men he had hired to clear the area with torches and axes, tearing down the vines and trees and brush that had covered the land for centuries, terrifying away the creatures who had made their homes inside amid the undergrowth..." Illustration by Sumit Roy

It was unclear how much time had passed, or even why she awoke at all, but she did indeed awaken, laying at the foot of a wooden structure that looked wholly unfamiliar – the beginnings of a house that the Montero family was building as their new home, and just a short walk away, they appeared to have attempted to save and replant the camellia tree. But its leaves had been all but ripped off, its blossoms crushed and leaving only a few errant buds. It was grotesque. It had been shoved into unfamiliar ground and forcibly ordered to take root, and to Camellia, it appeared nothing but a mockery. They had ripped something beautiful and thriving from the place where it belonged. They had kept it as a trophy as though this artificial existence meant that it was still truly alive. It was sickening, and Camellia knew then that this had destroyed a piece of her as well. Fleeing into shorn woods that had once been lush and lively, she ran furiously, calling out for her friend, pleading for Kawayan to answer, but also hoping that he too had gotten away.

She stopped only when she arrived in the space where the old bamboo grove had once been, now burnt to ruin and ash, still smoldering with no trace of life. Wherever Kawayan was, he was not here. For the first time, Camellia was truly alone.

It was in this moment, kneeling sorrowfully among the smoldering stubs of once proud bamboo shoots that her beloved friend had so lovingly tended, that Camellia looked to the sky and spoke a curse on Lucio Montero and all his progeny, an oath that just as he had wiped so many of the engkanto and the beings of this forest from existence, so too would he be erased from memory. His bloodline would end, or Camellia would not rest.

This was the promise she had made, the solemn contract she had sealed with the memory of all who had been lost, and for centuries, she had diligently kept it – and she realized now that outliving all she had known and loved, fueled only by regret and longing, was so deeply tiresome. Only did it now dawn on her how far removed she was from the joyful sprite that had lived once in the peaceful parcel of land across the sea. She had gone, and she could never return. She longed terribly for rest. If she could not see the beauty of her home again, hear the voices of her dear friends, feel the lifeblood of the untainted forest pulsing underfoot, she would settle for rest, but only when she could do so with the satisfaction that Rico Montero, the last of Lucio's bloodline, would not find peace.

She had taken on the ways they spoke and dressed and lived, changing herself decade after decade and was no more herself anymore than the shorn mass of flowerless limbs in the forest of her youth was the same lush camellia tree it had once been.

In the shadows of the razed forest clearing, Camellia watched as Lucio flattened the large parcel of land and sold the lumber and stone to amass a small fortune, enough to purchase a healthy berth of livestock. But the oxen never bore young that survived to adulthood, the chickens' eggs were devoured by creatures displaced from their forest homes.

"Of course you can feast on them," Camellia would whisper every night to the wild dogs as they gazed hungrily at the chicken coop behind the Montero home. "Hasn't this forest always given us everything we need to survive? Does it not belong to all of us, together? Go. Eat."

And even in her loneliness as the sole remaining

spirit of the old forest, the only surviving engkanto for miles, Camellia grew in her power, whispering nightly to the forest to never be tamed, to refuse to be owned or restricted by the hubris of Lucio Montero. When Montero tried to raise crops, Camellia whispered to their roots to refuse to take hold, and to the vines to crawl up from the ground and choke out the crops. Every attempt that Lucio made to milk the land for his own gain, Camellia met his efforts with what little force of nature she could still command, her anger fueled every day by the sight of the flowerless clipping of the camellia tree that they had forced to try and grow outside of its home soil, covered in only leaves that withered nearly as quickly as they grew.

She watched as Lucio, too, grew twisted and gnarled, embittered by failure after failure to make the land thrive under his control.

"Lucio, we have tried our best," his wife said. "You've done everything you can to make a living from this land, but *kung hindi talaga para sa atin*[6] —"

"This land is ours and it will do what we tell it to,"

---

[6] If it truly was not meant to be ours –

Lucio insisted. "It doesn't have a mind of its own. We own it, and it does what we say."

"When has that ever been true, Lucio? This land has never done as we demanded. We demand and we fight and we beg and plead, but it does nothing because it does not belong to us. If it did, would we be having this conversation right now? Lucio, this is *foolish*—"

And the sound of Lucio striking his wife hard across the cheek for the first time was carried on the wind to Camellia's ears. His apologies quickly followed, but it was in this moment that Camellia knew that Lucio's pride and his insistence on breaking the will of the land that belonged to him in deed only had corrupted him so that he valued this battle against the land above the family that relied on him.

The years passed, and the Monteros' young son grew, wed, and had a child of his own. Dutifully, this young man fought against the land in hopes of taming it the way he had grown up watching his father do. But unlike his father, he did not go to his grave tied inextricably to his pride. He too came to have a son, who himself had just married and was preparing to take on the responsibility of tending to the land when one evening, his father took him aside and slide an envelope of money into his hand as he walked into the bar, lamplit front room of their home after a day of struggling to find work to no avail. The young man, Francisco, looked down in confusion as he realized that there was a good sum of money in the envelope, and he looked up questioningly at his father.

"Pa?"

"I sold the land – everything but this small patch that your mother and I need to survive. I want you to take your wife and have your family somewhere you can live better than this – better than being a slave to the land that clearly doesn't want to be owned."

"You want us to leave?"

"I want you to live," he explained, the expression on his face that was weathered beyond its years soft but determined to ensure that his son would listen. "Your mother and I can live a humble life here, but we know you can have more."

And had Camellia, too, not been embittered by decades of fixation on the loss of her own home, and on her own loneliness, this may have been enough to convince her to leave the Montero family in peace. But one honorable act did not restore her home. It did not bring back Kawayan and the other spirits of the forest. Instead, it merely convinced Camellia to stay her hand, to follow Francisco as he complied with his father's instruction to take his family and build a life elsewhere – in a place across a vast ocean, where Francisco went from a young, struggling custodian to a revered detective in the city of M-Town. What right did they have to simply run away and start fresh in a new home, when the home of the spirits of the forest could never be restored?

But as bitter as she was, Camellia was not heartless or without pity, nor did she forget the commitment of her kind to protect those who were pure and kind. Detective Francisco Montero was so pure a soul that for decades, Camellia merely watched him from afar, taking on different names and identities and simply existing the way that people seemed to, so immersed in this new life that she surprised herself at how at times, she forgot the forest clearing and her home and her home and her dearest friend Kawayan. She had evaded notice so well all these years, she began to wonder if there were others like her that she passed on the street every day without ever even knowing.

Camellia would have even gone as far to call herself complacent in her life until for the first time – when Francisco and his son Monty first ate in the M-Town Diner and she heard the latter man speak – that again, Lucio's memory rumbled to the surface. Francisco, kind and principled, was simply an anomaly. Monty was proof, Camellia decided, that something corrupted at the root would continue to show the rot again and again until it was uprooted and destroyed at its source. Now after centuries, she would be able to say that she had succeeded.

Except, Camellia realized with a sinking feeling in her chest, that she had not taught him anything. This was nothing, this moment's pain that Monty was experiencing. Camellia did not put herself through a century of waiting and suffering for only a few moments of satisfaction. She realized only now that a fleeting sort of revenge would not bring her rest. She, in this body or any form she decided to take, could die over and over again, but this would still not be good enough for her to rest.

Camellia, in these final moments of clarity, recalled

that nothing had been so tiresome as living for centuries and simply watching all else age and wither and die away. It grew tiresome and even worse, felt like an imprisonment of its own sort to live forever and relive over and over again the pain of having to tear apart the life that was safe and familiar, alone – the same pain that had been the cause and the start of all this. This should never have been her pain to bear, Camellia thought bitterly. There could be no greater punishment. There was no more poetic means of fulfilling her purpose.

So now, even as all faded, even as the last wisps of life left this current form she had taken and kept for so long in pursuit of revenge, she could leave this body with satisfaction that her objective had been fulfilled – all of her years, she had been a being of her word and she was pleased that she had never allowed this to change.

Monty would be the last of Lucio Montero's progeny and his family line would end, wiped away and destroyed much like the tree whose destruction had spurred all of this into being. And Monty himself, for his brazen attack that led to the death of Camellia's current, transient form, would receive his recompense as well, but not with death.

With the last of her own strength, Camellia dragged herself over the floor to reach towards where Monty too lay dying, and she placed her hands on the wound on his stomach. The bleeding slowed and halted. The flesh sealed itself as though it had never been broken. And with a smile, for the very last time, Camellia shut the eyes of this form as the last of the life in her flowed into Monty. Lucio's punishment was completed, as was the punishment Camellia had for so long inflicted upon herself. It was time for Monty's to begin.

7 ❖ SO IT BEGINS

Monty wished he could have explained what happened the night he had intended to confront Camellia Ferrer, but explaining would have required him to remember, and this was simply something he could not do. Had he fallen asleep? He wasn't sure how that could have been possible, when he had been so full of adrenaline during his drive to meet her, he couldn't possibly have lost the rush so quickly. He remembered pulling up to the back entrance parking lot of the M-Town Diner, and he must have somehow fallen asleep – he would chalk it up to the fatigue from having been so relentless in his pursuit of answers in the Benny Salazar case. He did so, and to everyone he encountered this was a sufficient explanation – Monty had solved a major crime, and they all conceded that he was entitled to a little bit of brain fatigue after having pulled it off. They had seen his long hours poring over the boxes of evidence, his days of driving around chasing leads with relentless determination that they knew his father would have been proud of.

Admittedly, it made Monty feel a little sick – as much as he had convinced himself that the end would always justify the means, it was unsettling to be told he was finally living out his father's legacy when for reasons he could not put his finger on, he did not feel like he had succeeded yet. Detective Francisco Montero would not have considered this case solved, and he would not have rested. But, Monty had to remind himself, he was not his father. Perhaps the fact that he wanted to and tried to was the source of his unrest.

Whatever the case, Monty just remembered waking up in the morning still sitting in his car to a sore stomach – sore, as though from an old injury that was in the end stages of healing - a crick in his neck from the strange angle at which he must have dozed off, a locked up M-Town Diner, and the news that Camellia Ferrer had not shown up to work that morning. She did not arrive the next day, or the next. A check on her flat revealed no trace of her at all, everything remained undisturbed as though she had simply ceased to exist. That, however, was not something likely to happen. People didn't just disappear.

It only took a matter of days for Monty to realize that he simply had to come to grips with the fact that the trail ended here. The case was closed, Benny Salazar had committed all of the murders with his own two hands, had confessed to them, and no strange gut feeling about Camellia Ferrer, no suspicion of some strange, mystical, inexplicable connection could change this. This was fact, and this was all that Monty had, so even as he felt a nagging sense of failure knowing Benny Salazar – who was truth and repentant to the full extent that he could be – would live out the rest of his days in prison for his crimes, Monty would need to accept this. His father never would have. His father would have followed this gut feeling to the ends of the earth at the prospect of saving an innocent man.

But perhaps, Monty realized as he put the case file away for the last time and stared down at his empty desk, he could never be his father. It was dissatisfying, but it would pass. All things passed, Monty reminded himself. Everything was temporary.

EPILOGUE

Twenty-Five Years Prior

"Tell me a story, Pa!"

Young Rico Montero had climbed into his father's lap as he sat down in his old, worn out recliner in the sitting room of their small home. Detective Francisco Montero chuckled and shuffled so that his son could nestle in with him comfortably in the old blue chair — dark, navy suede that had required patching and scrubbing in some spots, and it had been a few years since the retractable foot rest had been able to open at all. Still, in spite of its age and obvious wear it was one of the few luxury items that Francisco had acquired for himself, with all the rest of the fruits of his labor being funneled towards a comfortable life for his wife and son. Even after a hard day's work, it was difficult to refuse his son's pleas for a story, knowing that it would not always be this way. A day would come, Francisco knew, that his son would cease to see the magic in his old stories. But that day had not yet arrived, and Francisco would resist its arrival indeed for as long as he possibly could.

"What story do you want to hear tonight, *anak*[7]?" Francisco asked, rocking gently in the chair as Rico squirmed to try and find a comfortable spot.

"I want to hear about where you grew up again," Rico replied immediately. "About the forest!"

"Alright, alright," Francisco chuckled in concession as though there were ever any doubt that he would give into his son's requests. "You remember I told you, when I was a boy, I lived far away from here, and our farmhouse was right next to a patch of old forest, with

---

7 Child, or son

trees taller than a lot of our buildings, and more flowers and fruits than we could ever name.."

"And there were creatures in the woods!" Rico blurted out excitedly, having heard all of these stories before but never having grown tired of them. "Like – like the half-horse, half-man!"

"The *tikbalang*[8]," Francisco agreed, reminding his son of the name in hopes that one day he would remember it all on his own. "Yes, they lived in the trees, and sometimes at night, we thought we could hear them, or smell them smoking their cigars out just beyond the tree line. And the *dwende*[9], who you always had to be careful not to disturb when you were walking deeper into the woods."

"Did you ever see any of them up close?" Rico asked, bouncing and squirming again to look up at his

---

[8] In Filipino folklore, the *tikbalang* is a creature whose appearance is part-horse, part-human – specifically, they have come to be known as having the head of a horse with long human limbs. These creatures are said to live among large trees in the forests of the Philippines, often also represented as protectors of the forest who play tricks on travelers through their territory.

[9] *Dwende* are creatures in folklore akin to dwarves said to live in the forest, often specifically in anthills. Their demeanor may range from benevolent, to mischievous, to even evil. Out of caution and respect, it is considered wise when walking through forest territory especially around ant hills or other formations they may inhabit to announce one's presence and ask for permission to pass, to prevent angering the small creatures and incurring punishment such as bad luck or illness.

father – little Rico was getting taller and heavier now, and his eager climbing on his father's lap occasionally made the older man wince at an errant knee to his stomach or elbow to his side, but he still could not bring himself to even suggest that perhaps his son was getting too big for this. Little boys, after all, only stayed little for such a short amount of time, and he wanted very much to keep his little boy this excited and full of wonder. "Did you ever talk to them? Were they good or bad?"

"They weren't good or bad. They just were. Just like people, we live our lives, and we have good moments, bad moments – that's part of being alive," Francisco said, raising a finger to his son's lips to hush him for a moment before the questions could continue in rapid fire. "I know they're real. One of them was in the forest near the home where I grew up I think I even spoke to her."

"What did she say?"

"She was the most beautiful woman – I saw her once when I was a boy, I ran too far into the woods and fell ad skinned my knee. And she appeared like a ghost out of the trees, like she had come out of nowhere. She asked if I wanted her to heal the scrape on my knee, and I told her no, it was fine. Then, she said if I followed her into the woods, she would give our family everything we ever dreamed," Francisco said. "She said that she would make the land burst forth with crops, and the animals would thrive, and we would have all the riches we ever dreamed of."

"And you said no? To all of that?" Rico asked shrilly, his eyes widening and his tiny fists gripping at his father's sleeves in disbelief while he rustled restlessly in his lap. "Pa, are you crazy?"

"I had to say no, *anak*. You don't accept gifts from the engkanto like that," Francisco said with a laugh, ruffling his son's hair. "Or else they own you. You become a spirit like them, too. Forever, until they're done with you. Everyone knows that. And who wants to live forever, anyway?"

ABOUT THE AUTHOR

Victoria Conlu is a registered nurse and an IT professional in South Texas, originally from the Bay Area in Northern California. She lives with her elementary school-age son, JB, and her grandmother. When not working or spending time with family, she enjoys crocheting and occasionally sells her crafts at local craft fairs. Writing, however, has been a passion since she was a child, and she takes joy in the fact that she has learned to leave room her life to share stories in a way that reaches a wide audience.

A LOOK AHEAD:
BAMBOO MAN

Senator Lorenzo Ka —

No. President Lorenzo Ka. He wasn't sure he would ever get used to this, but considering that he had just been sworn into office, he was going to have to try.

President Lorenzo Ka stood at the balcony of the Capitol building that would now be his home for at least the next four years, and he surveyed what he could of the outside world, of the country he was now tasked with governing. As his gaze passed over his surroundings, the cars and roads and buildings that practically scratched the sky, he could not help but remember how different this was from the life he had come from. Certainly, in the earliest of his memories, there was nothing like this. He had lived his earliest years deep in the countryside, in a place different from this bustling city, and there had been many times in his political career that he had wanted very much to pack up and return there, feeling like he did not belong here at all.

With thick, dark hair that swooped dramatically away from his face, tan skin, and almond shaped eyes, he had been made well aware that he did not look like the leaders his country had known for most of its history. Glancing back over his shoulder, he looked at the first thing he had hung up in his new home: a framed copy of a magazine article that had gone to print early in his presidential campaign with a headline that declared in large, bold letters: Bamboo Man – Can He Be Trusted With the Future of Our Nation?

Lorenzo chuckled a little and shook his head as he stared at it. He had since taken the term Bamboo Man and run with it, folding it into his campaign and leaning into all of its implications. The Bamboo Man had come to assume leadership of the free world, and for many, such a thing was unacceptable.

Yet here he was. Not Congressman Perry Owenthal, his fierce opponent with his blustering promises of prosperity and dominance over the rest of the world, his booming rhetoric, his staunch criticism of anyone who he deemed lazy and unworthy. The President of the United States was Lorenzo Ka, the softspoken Filipino American senator whose calm demeanor brought new justification to the term Bamboo Man, because of his ability to withstand Owenthal's blustering and bend without breaking, respond without snapping, like a grove of old bamboo.

He and a strong wave of support across the country had carried him definitively and with the utmost dignity into the highest office in the land, even amid jeers and criticism that he had no right, that he could not represent the people who had now become his constituents, because he did not look like them. On the campaign trail, he switched easily between the tongues of two homes – of the United States and the Philippines – and the presence of this foreign tongue in his campaign somehow seemed to instill fear.

What is he saying? Can he be trusted?

The questions were displayed across the screen over a clip of him praising a local Filipino restaurant at one of his stops along the campaign trail, with others guessing he was planning everything from election fraud to world domination.

And now that he was here, now that the first of the battles had been won, it all seemed so silly to Lorenzo who now was tasked with the bigger challenge of indeed being this man of two worlds. A presidential campaign was nothing compared to that.

He stepped out farther onto the balcony and out into the sun, taking a deep breath. The air here was fresh, but nonetheless had the distinct sense of city air. He hadn't breathed other air in so long, but remembered fondly how light it felt in one's lungs compared to city air. He shut his eyes and drew in a breath, as if to fill his lungs with the air he had at his disposal so that he could bring himself to love it just as much. He held the air in for a few seconds, then exhaled it in resignation as he realized he did not feel this fondness for it just yet. But it would come, he reassured himself. It had to.

"Mister President!"

The seconds that followed all seemed to be a blur –
there was the sound of someone from his security
detail calling out to him, a loud sound somewhere in
the distance that he could not quite identify, and just as
he was opening his eyes to try and gather what was
happening, a strange feeling in his chest that ripped
away the feeling of city air. He looked down and saw
blood beginning to soak into his shirt. Before he could
register any physical sensations, there was a sense of
weakness in his legs. Then, nothing…

☿

COMING SOON